W9-BIV-243

KAY THOMPSON'S ELOISE

Love & Kisses, Eloise

WITHDRAWN

STORY BY **Marc Cheshire**

ILLUSTRATED BY **Ted Enik**

Little Simon

NEW YORK · LONDON · TORONTO · SYDNEY

LITTLE SIMON

An imprint of Simon & Schuster Children's Publishing Division

1230 Avenue of the Americas, New York, New York 10020

Copyright © 2005 by the Estate of Kay Thompson

"Eloise" and related marks are trademarks of the Estate of Kay Thompson.

All rights reserved, including the right of reproduction in whole or in part in any form.

LITTLE SIMON is a registered trademark of Simon & Schuster, Inc.,

and associated colophon is a trademark of Simon & Schuster, Inc.

Manufactured in the United States of America

First Edition

2 4 6 8 10 9 7 5 3 1

ISBN 0-689-87156-2

It's almost Valentine's Day,
and Nanny says we must must must get ready.

MY VALENTINES

NANNY
WEENIE
SKIPPER DEE
LILY EMILY
VINCENT
TED
MR. SALOMONE
THOMAS
JOHANNA
JIMMY

Some people buy valentines at a store,

but I prefer to make my own.

"Come, come, my dear," says Nanny. "We must mail these cards so they will arrive by February 14th. You can deliver the rest by hand."

Today
I will *not* pour water
down the mail chute.

The best thing about Valentine's Day
is going to the candy store to get boxes of chocolate.

Nanny and I always get
a few extra boxes for ourselves.

When Valentine's Day finally comes
there is so much to do

that I don't know how I can possibly
get everything done!

I am all over the hotel
delivering valentines
and chocolate
and love love love
to absolutely everyone.

When I get hungry I go into the kitchen
to give the cooks their valentines
and get a little snack.

I like to watch the couples having romantic dinners in the Palm Court.

Sometimes people look like they need some help, so I play Cupid.

Mr. Salomone is often
not in a very good mood
when he sees me . . .

. . . but I tell him that on Valentine's Day you simply must be happy happy happy.

The last thing I do is give valentines to Weenie and Skipperdee . . .

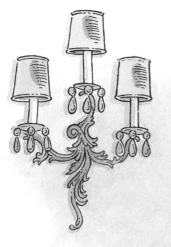

. . . and to Nanny,
who is my absolutely best friend
in the whole wide world!

No matter where she's off to, my mother always sends
the most beautiful roses and calls me long distance
to say how much she loves me, and we talk for a very
long time and charge it.

Ooooooooooooo,
I absolutely love Valentine's Day!